Poulet, Virginia

Blue Bug's
Christmas

BLUE BUG'S CHRISTMAS

By Virginia Poulet

Illustrated by Peggy Perry Anderson

CHILDRENS PRESS®

CHICAGO

For William and Mary Sowinski
on their 50th Anniversary!

Library of Congress Cataloging-in-Publication Data

Poulet, Virginia.
   Blue Bug's Christmas

   (Blue Bug books)
   Summary: Blue Bug and his friends choose and decorate
a tree for Christmas.
   [1.   Christmas—Fiction.   2.   Insects—Fiction]
I.   Anderson, Peggy Perry, ill.   II.   Title.
III.   Series: Poulet, Virginia. Blue Bug books.
PZ7.P86Bld   1987   [E]   87-15793
ISBN 0-516-03483-9

Childrens Press®, Chicago
Text copyright© 1987 by Virginia Maniglier-Poulet.
Illustrations copyright© 1987 by Regensteiner Publishing
   Enterprises, Inc.

The three friends

chose a tree

and hung lights,

ornaments, and

popcorn on a string.

They put up cards,

bells, and

stockings.

Nat painted toys.

Feebee made paper birds.

Blue Bug daydreamed.

They put straw

in the manger

and shined

a special star

for the tree top.